KU-515-287

Sharing Books From Birth to Five

Welcome to Practical Parenting Books

It's never too early to introduce a child to books. It's wonderful to see your baby gazing intently at a cloth book; your toddler poring over a favourite picture; or your older child listening quietly to a story. And you're his favourite storyteller, so have fun together while you're reading – use silly voices, linger over the pictures and leave pauses for your child to join in.

As you read *Ten Sleepy Bunnies*, enjoy the guessing and the spotting activities as well as the first counting rhymes. First name all the different animals and make their sounds, then point out the numbers at the bottom of the page. Don't forget to count the smaller creatures as well as the big ones!

Books open doors to other worlds, so take a few minutes out of your busy day to cuddle up close and lose yourselves in a story. Your child will love it – and so will you.

Jane & Clare

Jane Kemp Clare Walters

P.S. Look out, too, for *Tiny Trumpet*, the companion book in this age range, and all the other great books in the new Practical Parenting series.

AGE 2-3

This edition produced for The Book People Ltd, Hall Wood Avenue, Haydock, St Helens WA11 9UL

First published in Great Britain
by HarperCollins Publishers Ltd in 2000

3 5 7 9 10 8 6 4
ISBN: 0-00-764681-X

Text copyright © Jane Kemp and Clare Walters 2000
Illustrations copyright © Peter Curry 2000

The Practical Parenting/HarperCollins pre-school book series has been created by Jane Kemp and Clare Walters. The Practical Parenting imprimatur is used with permission by IPC Magazines Ltd.

Practical Parenting is published monthly by IPC Magazines Ltd. For subscription enquiries and orders, ring 01444 445555 or the credit card hotline (UK orders only) on 01622 778778.

The authors and illustrator assert the moral right to be identified as the authors and illustrator of the work.

A CIP catalogue record for this title is available from the British Library.

All rights reserved. No part of this publication may be reproduced, stored in a retrieval system, or transmitted in any form or by any means, electronic, mechanical, photocopying, recording or otherwise, without the prior permission of HarperCollins Publishers Ltd, 77-85 Fulham Palace Road, Hammersmith, London W6 8JB

The HarperCollins website address is: www.**fire**and**water**.com

Manufactured in China by Imago

Ten Sleepy Bunnies

Written by Jane Kemp and Clare Walters
Illustrated by Peter Curry

TED SMART

One busy mole

Digging underground,

Pops up her head

Guess who she's found?

1

one

Baa
baa

Two woolly sheep
Munching on the grass,
In the sky above
Who's flying past?

2

two

Three bright-eyed birds
Singing way up high,
On the branch below
Who scampers by?

3

three

Tweet
tweet

Chatter
chatter

Four cheeky squirrels
Clamber down the tree,
As they search for food
Who do they see?

4

four

Five dusty cows
Enjoy a long cool soak,
Down among the lilies
Can you hear a croak?

5

five

Moo
moo

Six leaping frogs
Catch fat flies for tea,
Ripples on the water
Who can that be?

6

six

Seven sparkling fish
Shimmer as they swim,
Over by the bank
Who waddles in?

7

seven

Quack
quack

Eight gliding ducks
Paddle in the reeds,
Which little animals
Are nibbling some seeds?

8

eight

Nine timid mice
Run beneath the gate,
Who's that hopping home
Now it's getting late?

9
nine

Squeak
squeak

Hop
hop

Ten sleepy bunnies
Yawn beneath the moon,
Night night, sleep tight,
Morning will come soon.

10

ten

Sharing Books From Birth to Five

£3.99
0 00 136130 9

£3.99
0 00 136132 5

AGE 0–1

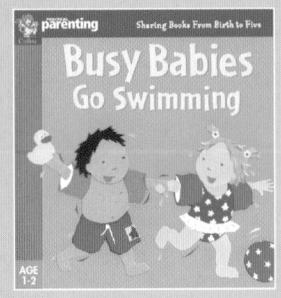

£3.99
0 00 136139 2

£3.99
0 00 136137 6

AGE 1–2

£3.99
0 00 136147 3

£3.99
0 00 136171 6

AGE 2–3

£3.99
0 00 136151 1

£3.99
0 00 136153 8

AGE 3–5

The Practical Parenting books are available from all good bookshops and can be ordered direct from HarperCollins Publishers by ringing 0141 7723200 and through the HarperCollins website: www.**fire**and**water**.com

You can also order any of these titles, with free post and packaging, from the Practical Parenting Bookshop on 01326 569339 or send your cheque or postal order together with your name and address to: Practical Parenting Bookshop, Freepost, PO Box 11, Falmouth, TR10 9EN.